The Trial of Love
Mary Shelley

www.novellix.se

First published in
The Keepsake, 1835

Published by Novellix, Stockholm, 2021

Cover image: GaryKillian/Shutterstock.com
Cover design & typeset: Lisa Benk
Printed & bound in: Latvia, Latgales Druka, 2020
ISBN: 978-91-7589-510-9

HAVING OBTAINED LEAVE from the Signora Priora to go out for a few hours, Angeline, who was a boarder at the convent of Sant' Anna, in the little town of Este, in Lombardy, set out on her visit. She was dressed with simplicity and taste; her faziola covered her head and shoulders; and from beneath, gleamed her large black eyes, which were singularly beautiful. And yet she was not, perhaps, strictly handsome; but, she had a brow smooth, open, and noble; a profusion of dark silken hair, and a clear, delicate, though brunette complexion. She had, too, an intelligent and thoughtful expression of countenance; her mind appeared often to commune with itself; and there was every token that she was deeply interested in, and often pleased with, the thoughts that filled it. She was of humble birth: her father had been steward to Count Moncenigo, a Venetian nobleman; her mother had been foster-mother to his only daughter. Both her parents were dead; they had left her comparatively rich; and she was a prize sought by all the young men of the class under nobility; but Angeline lived retired in her convent, and encouraged none of them.

She had not been outside its walls for many months; and she felt almost frightened as she found herself among the lanes that led beyond the town, and up the Euganean hills, to Villa Moncenigo, whither she was bending her steps. Every portion of the way was familiar to her. The Countess Moncenigo had died in childbirth of her second child, and from that time, Angeline's mother had lived at the villa. The family consisted of the Count, who was always, except during a few weeks in the autumn, at Venice, and the two children. Ludovico, the son, was early settled at Padua, for the sake of his education, and then Faustina only remained, who was five years younger than Angeline.

Faustina was the loveliest little thing in the world: unlike an Italian, she had laughing blue eyes, a brilliant complexion, and auburn hair; she had a sylph-like form, slender, round, and springy; she was very pretty, and vivacious, and self-willed, with a thousand winning ways, that rendered it delightful to yield to her. Angeline was like an elder sister: she waited on Faustina; she yielded to her in every thing; a word or smile of hers, was all-powerful. "I love her too much," she would sometimes say; "but I would endure any misery rather than see a tear in her eye." It was Angeline's character to concentrate her feelings, and to nurse them till they became passions; while excellent principles, and the sincerest piety, prevented her from being led astray by them.

Three years before, Angeline had, by the death of her mother, been left quite an orphan, and she and Faustina went to live at the convent of Sant' Anna, in the town of Este; but a year after, Faustina, then fifteen, was sent to complete her education at a very celebrated convent in Venice, whose aristocratic doors were closed against her ignoble companion. Now, at the age of seventeen, having finished her education, she returned home, and came to Villa Moncenigo with her father, to pass the months of September and October. They arrived this very night, and Angeline was on her way from her convent, to see and embrace her dearest companion.

There was something maternal in Angeline's

feelings – five years makes a considerable difference at the ages of ten to fifteen, and much, at seventeen and two-and-twenty. "The dear child," thought Angeline, as she walked along, "she must be grown taller, and, I dare say, more beautiful than ever. How I long to see her, with her sweet arch smile! I wonder if she found anyone at her Venetian convent to humour and spoil her, as I did here – to take the blame of her faults, and indulge her in her caprices. Ah! those days are gone! – she will be thinking now of becoming a sposa. I wonder if she has felt any thing of love." Angeline sighed. "I shall hear all about it soon – she will tell me everything, I am sure. – And I wish I might tell her – secrecy and mystery are so very hateful; but I must keep my vow, and in a month it will be all over – in a month I shall know my fate. In a month! – shall I see him then? – shall I ever see him again! But I will not think of that, I will only think of Faustina – sweet, beloved Faustina!"

And now Angeline was toiling up the hill side; she heard her name called; and on the terrace that overlooked the road, leaning over the balustrade, was the dear object of her thoughts – the pretty Faustina, the little fairy girl, blooming in youth, and smiling with happiness. Angeline's heart warmed to her with redoubled fondness.

Soon they were in each other's arms; and Faustina laughed, and her eyes sparkled, and she began to relate all the events of her two years' life, and showed herself as self-willed, childish, and yet as engaging and caressing as ever. Angeline listened with delight, gazed on her dimpled cheeks, sparkling eyes, and graceful gestures, in a perfect, though silent, transport of admiration. She would have had no time to tell her own story, had she been so inclined, Faustina talked so fast.

"Do you know, Angelinetta mia," said she, "I am to become a sposa this winter?"

"And who is the Signor Sposino?"

"I don't know yet; but during next carnival he is to be found. He must be very rich and very noble, papa says; and I say he must be very young and very good-tempered, and give me my own way, as you have always done, Angelina carina."

At length Angeline rose to take leave. Faustina did not like her going – she wanted her to stay all night – she would send to the convent to get the Priora's leave; but Angeline knowing that this was not to be obtained, was resolved to go, and at last, persuaded her friend to consent to her departure. The next day, Faustina would come herself to the convent to pay her old friends a visit, and Angeline could return with her in the evening, if the Priora would allow it. When this plan had been discussed and arranged, with one more embrace, they separated; and, tripping down the road, Angeline looked up, and Faustina looked down from the terrace, and waved her hand to her and smiled. Angeline was delighted with her kindness, her loveliness, the animation and sprightliness of her manner and conversation. She thought of her, at first, to the exclusion of every other idea, till, at a turn in the road, some circumstance recalled her thoughts to herself. "O, how too happy I shall be," she thought, "if he proves to be true! – with Faustina and Ippolito, life will be Paradise!" And then she traced back in her faithful memory, all that had occurred during the last two years. In the briefest possible way, we must do the same.

Faustina had gone to Venice, and Angeline was left alone in her convent. Though she did not much attach herself to anyone, she became intimate with Camilla della Toretta, a young lady from Bologna. Camilla's brother came to see her, and Angeline accompanied her in the parlour to receive his visit. Ippolito fell desperately in love, and Angeline was wont to return his affection. All her feelings were earnest and passionate; and yet, she could regulate their effects, and her conduct was irreproachable. Ippolito, on the contrary, was fiery and impetuous: he loved ardently, and could brook no opposition to the fulfilment of his wishes. He resolved on marriage, but being noble, feared his father's disapprobation: still it was necessary to seek his consent; and the old aristocrat, full of alarm and indignation, came to Este, resolved to use every measure to separate the lovers for ever. The gentleness and goodness of Angeline softened his anger, and his son's despair moved his compassion. He disapproved of the marriage, yet he could not wonder that Ippolito desired to unite himself to so much beauty and sweetness: and then, again, he reflected, that his son was very young, and might change his mind, and reproach him for his too easy acquiescence. He therefore made a compromise; he would give his consent in one year from that time, provided the young pair would engage themselves, by the most solemn oath, not to hold any communication by speech or letter during that interval. It was understood that this was to be a year of trial; that no engagement was to be considered to subsist until its expiration; when, if they continued faithful, their constancy would meet its reward. No doubt the father supposed, and even hoped, that, during their absence, Ippolito would change his sentiments, and form a more suitable attachment.

Kneeling before the cross, the lovers engaged themselves to one year of silence and separation; Angeline, with her eyes lighted up by gratitude and hope; Ippolito, full of rage and despair at this interruption to his felicity, to which he never would have assented, had not Angeline used every persuasion, every command, to instigate him to compliance; declaring, that unless he obeyed his father, she would seclude herself in her cell, and spontaneously become a prisoner, until the termination of the prescribed period. Ippolito took the vow, therefore, and immediately after set out for Paris.

One month only was now wanting before the year should have expired; and it cannot be wondered that Angeline's thoughts wandered from her sweet Faustina, to dwell on her own fate. Joined to the vow of absence, had been a promise to keep their attachment, and all concerning it, a profound secret from every human being, during the same term. Angeline consented readily (for her friend was away) not to come back till the stipulated period; but the latter had returned, and now, the concealment weighed on Angeline's conscience: there was no help – she must keep her word.

With all these thoughts occupying her, she had reached the foot of the hill, and was ascending again the one on which the town of Este stands, when she heard a rustling in the vineyard that bordered one side of the road – footsteps – and a well-known voice speaking her name.

"Santa Vergine! Ippolito!" she exclaimed, "is this your promise?"

"And is this your reception of me?" he replied, reproachfully. "Unkind one! because I am not cold enough to stay away – because this last month was an intolerable eternity, you turn from me – you wish me gone. It is true, then, what I have heard – you love another! Ah! my journey will not be fruitless – I shall learn who he is, and revenge your falsehood."

Angeline darted a glance full of wonder and

reproach; but she was silent, and continued her way. It was in her heart not to break her vow, and so to draw down the curse of heaven on their attachment. She resolved not to be induced to say another word; and, by her steady adherence to her oath, to obtain forgiveness for his infringement. She walked very quickly, feeling happy and miserable at the same time – and yet not so – happiness was the genuine, engrossing sentiment; but she feared, partly her lover's anger, and more, the dreadful consequences that might ensue from his breach of his solemn vow. Her eyes were radiant with love and joy, but her lips seemed glued together; and resolved not to speak, she drew her faziola close round her face, that he might not even see it, as she walked speedily on, her eyes fixed on the ground. Burning with rage, pouring forth torrents of reproaches, Ippolito kept close to her side – now reproaching her for infidelity – now swearing revenge – now describing and lauding his own constancy and immutable love. It was a pleasant, though a dangerous theme. Angeline was tempted a thousand times to reward him by declaring her own unaltered feelings; but she overcame the desire, and, taking her rosary in her hand, began to tell her beads. They drew near the town, and finding that she was not to be persuaded, Ippolito at length left her, with protestations that he would discover his rival, and take vengeance on him for her cruelty and indifference. Angeline entered her convent, hurried into her cell – threw herself on her knees – prayed God to forgive her lover for breaking his vow; and then, overcome with joy at the proof he had given of his constancy, and of the near prospect of their perfect happiness, her head sank on her arms, and she continued absorbed in a reverie which bore the very hues of heaven. It had been a bitter struggle to withstand his entreaties, but her doubts were dissipated, he was true, and at the appointed hour would claim her; and she who had loved through the long year with such fervent, though silent, devotion, would be rewarded! She felt secure – thankful to heaven – happy. – Poor Angeline!

The next day, Faustina came to the convent: the nuns all crowded round her. *"Quanto è hellina,"* cried one. *"E tanta carina!"* cried another. *"S' è fatta la sposina?"* – "Are you betrothed yet?" asked a third. Faustina answered with smiles and caresses, and innocent jokes and laughter. The nuns idolized her; and Angeline stood by, admiring her lovely friend, and enjoying the praises lavished on her. At length, Faustina must return; and Angeline, as anticipated, was permitted to accompany her.

"She might go to the villa with her," the Priora said, "but not stay all night – it was against the rules."

Faustina entreated, scolded, coaxed, and at length succeeded in persuading the superior to allow her friend's absence for a single night. They then commenced their return together, attended by a maid servant – a sort of old duenna. As they walked along, a cavalier passed them on horseback.

"How handsome he is!" cried Faustina: "who can he be?"

Angeline blushed deeply, for she saw that it was Ippolito. He passed on swiftly, and was soon out of sight. They were now ascending the hill, the villa almost in sight, when they were alarmed by a bellowing, a hallooing, a shrieking, and a bawling, as if a den of wild beasts, or a madhouse, or rather both together, had broken loose. Faustina turned pale; and soon her companion was equally frightened, for a buffalo, escaped from the yoke, was seen tearing down the hill, filling the air with their roars, and a whole troop of *contadini* after him, screaming and shrieking – he was exactly in the path of the friends. The old duenna cried out, *"O, Gesu Maria!"*

and fell flat on the earth. Faustina uttered a piercing shriek, and caught Angeline round the waist; who threw herself before the terrified girl, resolved to suffer the danger herself, rather than it should meet her friend – the animal was close upon them. At that moment, the cavalier rode down the hill, passing the buffalo, and then, wheeling round, intrepidly confronted the wild animal. With a ferocious bellow he swerved aside, and turned down a lane that opened to the left; but the horse, frightened, reared, threw his rider, and then galloped down the hill. The cavalier lay motionless, stretched on the earth.

It was now Angeline's turn to scream; and she and Faustina both anxiously ran to their preserver. While the latter fanned him with her large green fan, which Italian ladies carry to make use of as a parasol, Angeline hurried to fetch some water. In a minute or two, colour revisited his cheeks, and he opened his eyes; he saw the beautiful Faustina, and tried to rise. Angeline at this moment arrived, and presenting the water in a bit of gourd, put it to his lips – he pressed her hand – she drew it away. By this time, old Caterina, finding all quiet, began to look about her, and seeing only the two girls hovering over a fallen man, rose and drew near.

"You are dying!" cried Faustina: "you have saved my life, and are killed yourself."

Ippolito tried to smile. "I am not dying," he said, "but I am hurt."

"Where? how?" cried Angeline. "Dear Faustina, let us send for a carriage for him, and take him to the villa."

"O! yes," said Faustina: "go, Caterina – run – tell papa what has happened – that a young cavalier has killed himself in saving my life."

"Not killed myself," interrupted Ippolito; "only broken my arm, and, I almost fear, my leg."

Angeline grew deadly pale, and sank on the ground.

"And you will die before we get help," said Faustina; "that stupid Caterina craws like a snail."

"I will go to the villa," cried Angeline, "Caterina shall stay with you and Ip – *Buon dio*! what am I saying?"

She rushed away, and left Faustina fanning her lover, who again grew very faint. The villa was soon alarmed, the Signor Conte sent off for a surgeon, and caused a mattress to be slung, with four men to carry it, and came to the assistance of Ippolito. Angeline remained in the house; she yielded at last to her agitation, and wept bitterly, from the effects of fright and grief. "O that he should break his vow thus to be punished – would that the atonement had fallen upon me!" Soon she roused herself, however, prepared the bed, sought what bandages she thought might be necessary, and by that time he had been brought in. Soon after the surgeon came; he found that the left arm was certainly broken, but the leg was only bruised: he then set the limb, bled him, and giving him a composing draught, ordered that he should be kept very quiet. Angeline watched by him all night, but he slept soundly, and was not aware of her presence. Never had she loved so much. His misfortune, which was accidental, she took as a tribute of his affection, and gazed on his handsome countenance, composed in sleep, thinking, "Heaven preserve the truest lover that ever blessed a maiden's vows!"

The next morning Ippolito woke without fever and in good spirits. The contusion on his leg was almost nothing; he wanted to rise: the surgeon visited him, and implored him to remain quiet only a day or two to prevent fever, and promised a speedy cure if he would implicitly obey his mandates. Angeline spent the day at the villa, but would not see him again. Faustina talked incessantly of his courage, his gallantry, his engaging manners. She was the heroine of the story.

It was for her that the cavalier had risked his life; her he had saved. Angeline smiled a little at her egotism. "It would mortify her if I told her the truth," she thought: so she remained silent. In the evening it was necessary to return to the convent; should she go in and say adieu to Ippolito? Was it right? Was it not breaking her vow? Still how could she resist? She entered and approached him softly; he heard her step, and looked up eagerly, and then seemed a little disappointed.

"Adieu! Ippolito," said Angeline, "I must go back to my convent. If you should become worse, which heaven forbid, I will return to wait on you, nurse you, die with you; if you get well, as with God's blessing there seems every hope, in one short month, I will thank you as you deserve. Adieu! dear Ippolito."

"Adieu! dear Angeline; you mean all that is right, and your conscience approves you: do not fear for me. I feel health and strength in my frame, and I bless the inconvenience and pain I suffer since you and your sweet friend are safe. Adieu! Yet, Angeline, one word: – my father, I hear, took Camilla back to Bologna with him last year – perhaps you correspond?"

"You mistake; by the Marchese's desire, no letters have passed."

"And you have obeyed in friendship as in love – you are very good. Now I ask a promise also – will you keep one to me as well as to my father?"

"If it be nothing against our vow."

"Our vow! you little nun – are our vows so mighty? – No, nothing against our vow; only that you will not write to Camilla nor my father, nor let this accident be known to them; it would occasion anxiety to no purpose: – will you promise?"

"I will promise not to write without your permission."

"And I rely on you keeping your word as you have your vow. Adieu, Angeline. What! go without one kiss?"

She ran out of the room, not to be tempted; for compliance with this request would have been a worse infringement of her engagement than any she had yet perpetrated.

She returned to Este, anxious, yet happy; secure in her lover's faith, and praying fervently that he might speedily recover. For several days after, she regularly went to Villa Moncenigo to ask after him, and heard that he was getting progressively well, and at last she was informed that he was permitted to leave his room. Faustina told her this, her eyes sparkling with delight. She talked a great deal of her cavalier, as she called him, and her gratitude and admiration. Each day, accompanied by her father, she had visited him, and she had always some new tale to repeat of his wit, his elegance, and his agreeable compliments. Now he was able to join them in the saloon, she was doubly happy. Angeline, after receiving this information, abstained from her daily visit, since it could no longer be paid without subjecting her to the risk of encountering her lover. She sent each day, and heard of his recovery; and each day she received messages from her friend, inviting her to come. But she was firm – she felt that she was doing right; and though she feared that he was angry, she knew that in less than a fortnight, to such had the month decreased since she first saw him, she could display her real sentiments, and as he loved her, he would readily forgive. Her heart was light, or full only of gratitude and happiness.

Each day, Faustina entreated her to come, and her entreaties became more urgent, while still Angeline excused herself. One morning her young friend rushed into her cell to reproach, and question, and wonder at her absence. Angeline was obliged to promise to go; and then she asked about the cavalier, to discover how she might so time her visit, as to avoid seeing him. Faustina blushed – a charming confusion overspread her face as she cried, "O, Angeline! it is for his sake I wish you to come."

Angeline blushed now in her turn, fearing that her secret was betrayed, and asked hastily, "What has he said?"

"Nothing," replied her vivacious friend; "and that is why I need you. O, Angeline, yesterday, papa asked me how I liked him, and added that if his father consented, he saw no reason why we should not marry – Nor do I – and yet, does he love me? O, if he does not love me, I would not have a word said, nor his father asked – I would not marry him for the world!" and tears sprung into the sensitive girl's eyes, and she threw herself into Angeline's arms.

"Poor Faustina," thought Angeline, "are you to suffer through me?" and she caressed and kissed her with soothing fondness. Faustina continued. She felt sure, she said, that Ippolito did love her. The name fell startlingly on Angeline's ear, thus pronounced by another; and she turned pale and trembled, while she struggled not to betray herself. The tokens of love he gave were not much, yet he looked so happy when she came in, and pressed her so often to remain – and then his eyes –

"Does he ever ask anything about me?" said Angeline.

"No – why should he?" replied Faustina.

"He saved my life," the other answered, blushing.

"Did he – when? – O, I remember; I only thought of mine; to be sure, your danger was as great – nay, greater, for you threw yourself before me. My own dearest friend, I am not ungrateful, though Ippolito renders me forgetful."

All this surprised, nay, stunned Angeline. She did not doubt her lover's fidelity, but she feared for her friend's happiness, and every idea gave way to that – She promised to pay her a visit, that very evening.

And now, see her again walking slowly up the hill, with a heavy heart on Faustina's account, and hoping that her love, sudden and unreturned, would not involve her future happiness. At the turn of the road near the villa, her name was called, and she looked up, and again bending from the balustrade, she saw the smiling face of her pretty friend; and Ippolito beside her. He started and drew back as he met her eyes. Angeline had come with a resolve to put him on his guard, and was reflecting how she could speak so as not to compromise her friend. It was labour lost; Ippolito was gone when she entered the saloon, and did not appear again. "He would keep his vow," thought Angeline; but she was cruelly disturbed on her friend's account, and she knew not what to do. Faustina could only talk of her cavalier. Angeline felt conscience-stricken; and totally at loss how to act. Should she reveal her situation to her friend? That, perhaps, was best, and yet she felt it most difficult of all; besides, sometimes she almost suspected that Ippolito had become unfaithful. The thought came with a spasm of agony, and went again; still it unhinged her, and she was unable to command her voice. She returned to her convent, more unquiet, more distressed than ever.

Twice she visited the villa, and still Ippolito avoided her, and Faustina's account of his behaviour to her, grew more inexplicable. Again and again, the fear that she had lost him, made her sick at heart; and again she reassured herself that his avoidance and silence towards her resulted from his vow, and that hist mysterious conduct towards Faustina existed only in the lively girl's imagination. She meditated continually on the part she ought to take, while appetite and sleep failed her; at length she grew too ill to visit the villa, and for two days, was confined to her bed. During the feverish hours that now passed, unable to move, and miserable at the thought of Faustina's fate, she came to a resolve to write to Ippolito. He would not see her, so she had no other means of communication. Her vow forbade the act; but that was already broken in so many ways; and now she acted without a thought of self; for her dear friend's sake only. But, then, if her letter should get into the hands of others; if Ippolito meant to desert her for Faustina? – then her secret should be buried forever in her own heart. She therefore resolved to write so that her letter would not betray her to a third person. It was a task of difficulty. At last it was accomplished.

"The signor cavaliere would excuse her, she hoped. She was – she had ever been as a mother to the Signorina Faustina – she loved her more than her life. The signor cavaliere was acting, perhaps, a thoughtless part. – Did he understand? – and though he meant nothing, the world would conjecture. All she asked was, for his permission to write to his father, that this state of mystery and uncertainty might end as speedily as possible."

She tore ten notes – was dissatisfied with this, yet sealed it, and crawling out of her bed, immediately despatched it by the post.

This decisive act calmed her mind, and her health felt the benefit. The next day, she was so well that she resolved to go up to the villa, to discover what effect her letter had created. With a beating heart she ascended the lane, and at the accustomed turn looked up. No Faustina was watching. That was not strange, since she was not expected; and yet, she knew not why, she felt miserable: tears started into her eyes. "If I could only see Ippolito for one minute – obtain the slightest explanation, all would be well!"

Thinking thus, she arrived at the villa, and entered the saloon. She heard quick steps, as of some one retreating as she came in. Faustina was seated at a table reading a letter – her cheeks flushed, her bosom heaving with agitation. Ippolito's hat and cloak were near her, and betrayed that he had just left the room in haste. She turned – she saw Angeline – her eyes flashed fire – she threw the letter she had been reading at her friend's feet; Angelina saw that it was her own.

"Take it!" said Faustina: "it is yours. Why you wrote it – what it means – I do not ask: it was at least indelicate, and, I assure you, useless – I am not one to give my heart unasked, nor to be refused when proposed by my father. Take up your letter,

Angeline. O, I could not believe that you would have acted thus by me!"

Angeline stood as if listening, but she heard not a word; she was motionless – her hands clasped, her eyes swimming with tears, fixed on her letter.

"Take it up, I say," said Faustina, impatiently stamping with her little foot; "it came too late, whatever your meaning was. Ippolito has written to his father for his consent to marry me; my father has written also." Angeline now started and gazed wildly on her friend.

"It is true! Do you doubt – shall I call Ippolito to confirm my words?" Faustina spoke exultingly. Angeline struck – terrified – hastily took up the letter, and without a word turned away, left the saloon – the house, descended the hill, and returned to her convent. Her heart bursting, on fire, she felt as if her frame was possessed of a spirit not her own: she shed no tears, but her eyes were starting from her head – convulsive spasms shook her limbs; she rushed into her cell – threw herself on the floor, and then she could weep – and after torrents of tears, she could pray, and then – think again her dream of happiness was ended forever, and wish for death.

The next morning, she opened her unwilling eyes to the light, and rose. It was day; and all must rise to live through the day, and she among the rest, though the sun shone not for her as before, and misery converted life into torture. Soon she was startled by the intelligence that a cavalier was in the parlour desirous of seeing her. She shrunk gloomily within herself, and refused to go down. The portress returned a quarter of an hour after. He was gone, but had written to her; and she delivered the letter. It lay on the table before Angeline – she cared not to open it – all was over, and needed not this confirmation. At length, slowly, and with an effort, she broke the seal. The date was the anniversary of the expiration of the year. Her tears burst forth; and then a cruel hope was born in her heart that all was a dream, and that now, the Trial of Love being at an end, he had written to claim her. Instigated by this deceitful suggestion, she wiped her eyes, and read these words:

"I am come to excuse myself from an act of baseness. You refuse to see me, and I write; for, unworthy as I must ever be in your eyes, I would not appear worse than I am. I received your letter in Faustina's presence – she recognized your handwriting. You know her wilfulness, her impetuosity; she took it from me, and I could not prevent her. I will say no more. You must hate me; yet rather afford me your pity, for I am miserable. My honour is now engaged; it was all done almost before I knew the danger – but there is no help – I shall know no peace till you forgive me, and yet I deserve your curse. Faustina is ignorant of our secret. Farewell." The paper dropped from Angeline's hand.

It was vain to describe the variety of grief that the poor girl endured. Her piety, her resignation, her noble, generous nature came to her assistance, and supported her when she felt that without them, she must have died. Faustina wrote to say that she would have seen her, but that Ippolito was averse from her doing so. The answer had come from the Marchese della Toretta – a glad consent; but he was ill, and they were all going to Bologna; on their return they would meet.

This departure was some comfort to the unfortunate girl. And soon another came in the shape of a letter from Ippolito's father, full of praises for her conduct. His son had confessed all to him, he said; she was an angel – heaven would reward her, and still greater would be her recompense, if she would deign to forgive her faithless lover. Angeline found relief in answering this letter, and pouring forth a part of the weight of grief and thought that burthened her. She forgave him freely, and prayed that he and his lovely bride might enjoy every blessing.

Ippolito and Faustina were married, and spent two or three years in Paris and the south of Italy. She had been ecstatically happy at first; but soon the rough world, and her husband's light, inconstant nature inflicted a thousand wounds in her young bosom. She longed for the friendship, the kind sympathy of Angeline; to repose her head on her soft heart, and to be comforted. She proposed a visit to Venice – Ippolito consented – and they visited Este in their way. Angeline had taken the veil in the convent of Sant' Anna. She was cheerful, if not happy; she listened in astonishment to Faustina's sorrows, and strove to console her. Ippolito, also, she saw with calm and altered feelings; he was not the being her soul had loved; and if she had married him, with her deep feelings, and exalted ideas of honour, she felt that she should have been even more dissatisfied than Faustina.

The couple lived the usual life of Italian husband and wife. He was gay, inconstant, careless; she consoled herself with a cavaliere servente. Angeline, dedicated to heaven, wondered at all these things; and how any could so easily make transfer of affections, which with her, were sacred and immutable.